The COOL CRAZY CRICKETS CLUB

Leo

Miranda

Noodles

Marcus

Phoebe

DAVID ELLIOTT

ILLUSTRATED BY PAUL MEISEL

CANDLEWICK PRESS

For my mother,
Martha Melissa Elliott
D. E.

For my "cool crickets," Peter, Alex, and Andrew
P. M.

First paperback edition in this format 2010

The Library of Congress has cataloged the hardcover edition as follows:

Elliott, David (David A.)
The Cool Crazy Crickets Club / David Elliott ; illustrated by Paul Meisel. —1st ed.
p. cm.
Summary: Follows the humorous activities of four friends and a dog as they find
a name, meeting place, mascot, and purpose for their new club.
ISBN 978-0-7636-0601-5 (hardcover)
[1. Clubs—Fiction.] I. Meisel, Paul, ill. II. Title.
PZ7.E447Co 2000
[E] — dc21 99-043676
ISBN 978-0-7636-1403-4 (paperback)
ISBN 978-0-7636-4659-2 (reformatted paperback)

10 11 12 13 14 15 16 CCP 10 9 8 7 6 5 4 3 2 1

Printed in Shenzhen, Guangdong, China

This book was typeset in Usherwood and Tempus Sans.
The illustrations were done in watercolor and ink.

Candlewick Press
99 Dover Street
Somerville, Massachusetts 02144

visit us at www.candlewick.com

CONTENTS

(cricket)

CHAPTER 1

The Club Gets a Name

It was a hot summer day. Leo and Marcus were sitting on Leo's front porch with Leo's dog, Noodles. They were swinging in a big wooden swing.

"Let's start a club," said Leo.

"Okay," said Marcus. "Who will be in the club?"

"You and me," answered Leo.

"A two-person club?" said Marcus.

"Make that a four-person club," said Phoebe, as she and Miranda stepped onto the porch.

"We want to be in the club," said Phoebe. "Right, Miranda?"

"Right! If there is a club, we're in it," Miranda answered.

"Better let them in," Marcus said.

"Okay," Leo said. "You're in the club."

"Of course we are," Miranda said. "We already told you that."

"We are also in the swing," said Phoebe. "Move over."

"What's the name of the club?" asked Miranda. "A club should have a name."

"I have a good name for us," said Marcus. "The Doodles!"

"The Doodles?" said Miranda. "I don't want to be a Doodle."

"Neither do I," Phoebe said. "I want to be a Piñata. Let's name our club the Piñatas."

"People hit piñatas with big sticks," said Leo. "If we call ourselves the Piñatas, people might hit us."

Just then, from under the porch, a cricket began to sing. The cricket gave Phoebe an idea.

"That's it!" she shouted. "That's the name for us! The Crickets!"

"The Crickets?" Leo said. "If we name our club the Crickets, I'm quitting."

"Me, too," said Marcus. "We want a cool name for our club. Not some dumb name like the Crickets."

"How about the Cool Crickets, then?" said Phoebe.

"That's crazy," said Leo.

"How about the Cool *Crazy* Crickets, then?" said Miranda.

"The Cool Crazy Crickets," repeated Marcus. "I like it!"

"Me, too," said Phoebe. "The Cool Crazy Crickets!"

Leo was silent. He looked at his friends.

Suddenly, he jumped high in the air.

"I'm cool!" he shouted. "I'm crazy!
I'm a Cool Crazy Cricket!"
And that's how the club got its name.

CHAPTER 2

The Club Gets a Clubhouse

It was the first meeting of the club. Leo was worried.

"We have a big problem," he said to the other Cool Crazy Crickets. "We have a club, but we don't have a clubhouse. Every club needs a clubhouse."

"That's not a problem," said Phoebe.
"We can use my room."

The Cool Crazy Crickets ran to
Phoebe's house.

They ran in the door.

They ran down the hall.

When they got to Phoebe's room, they stopped running.

"Welcome to our new clubhouse!"
Phoebe called.

"Don't you ever clean your room?"
asked Miranda.

"Sure," Phoebe said. "I just cleaned it
this morning."

"Let's go to my room," said Marcus.

Marcus's room was very nice.
It wasn't at all like Phoebe's.
It also wasn't empty.
"Oh no!" Miranda said.
"O NO!" yelled the little boy.

"It's your little brother, Teddy!" said Leo.

"ME TEDDY!" Teddy yelled.

Teddy was little, but Teddy was loud.

"Don't pay any attention to him," said Marcus. "He's just a baby."

"JUT BAY BEE!" yelled Teddy.

"Does he ever stop yelling?" asked Phoebe.

"When he's sleeping," said Marcus.

"WEN SWEE PING!" yelled Teddy.

"Yow!" said Leo. "Let's get out of here."

"OW DA HEER!" Teddy yelled.

The Crickets ran back to Leo's yard.

"Finding a clubhouse isn't going to be easy," said Miranda.

Just then, a big truck stopped in front of Leo's house. Two men got out of the truck.

"Is this 52 Prince Street?" asked the driver.

"Yes," said Leo.

"Well, your new refrigerator is here," said the man.

The Cool Crazy Crickets watched as the men moved a big box off the truck.

"Wow!" said Marcus. "That box is almost as big as a house!"

"Hey, it could be our clubhouse!" cried Leo.

"It's kind of small for four people," said Phoebe.

"We have another empty box in the truck," said the driver. "You can have that one, too."

For the next two hours, the Cool Crazy Crickets were very busy, cutting and taping and painting.

Leo made a secret entrance and a special door for Noodles.

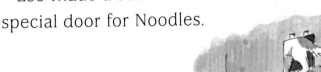

 Phoebe made a peephole.

Miranda made the clubhouse beautiful.

Marcus made a booby trap to keep out spies. Even Noodles helped.

Finally, the clubhouse was finished.
"It's fantastic!" said Leo.
"It's stupendous!" said Phoebe.
"It's incredible!" said Miranda.
"It's ours!" said Marcus.
The Cool Crazy Crickets
went inside.

Leo began to laugh.

"Do you know why this is the perfect clubhouse for us?" he asked.

"Why?" asked the other Crickets.

"Well, this is a *refrigerator* box, isn't it?" asked Leo.

"Yes," said Phoebe. "So?"

"So," said Leo, "we are the *Cool* Crazy Crickets, aren't we?"

CHAPTER 3

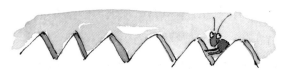

The Club Gets a Mascot

The next day, Marcus, Phoebe, and Miranda were sitting in their new clubhouse. Leo came in through the secret entrance.

"Where were you?" asked Marcus. "We've been waiting for you."

"I had to take care of Noodles," said Leo. "I had to feed him and give him water and take him for a walk."

"I've called this meeting of the club," said Leo, "because we have another problem."

"What is it this time?" asked Miranda.

"We need a mascot," said Leo. "Every club should have a mascot."

"A mask? Why do we need a mask?" asked Marcus. "Is this a Halloween club?"

"Let's call ourselves the Trick or Treaters!" said Phoebe.

"Not a mask," said Leo. "A *mascot*."

"Yes, we need a mascot!" said Phoebe. "Uh, what's a mascot?"

"A mascot brings good luck," Leo said. "It's usually some kind of animal."

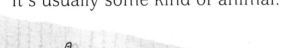

Suddenly, Noodles sat up.

He was an animal.

He could be a mascot!

Noodles looked straight at Miranda.

"I have it!" she said. "I know the perfect mascot!"

"Let's guess who it is," said Leo.

"Okay," said Miranda. "Here's a clue.
He is very beautiful."

Noodles cocked his ears.
He gazed at Phoebe
with his big, brown,
beautiful eyes.

"I know who it is!" Phoebe shouted.
"And Miranda is right. He is
the perfect mascot for us."

"Don't tell us yet," said Leo.
"Give us another clue."

"Okay," said Phoebe. "He is also very friendly." Noodles wagged his tail and licked Marcus's face.

"I know who it is!" Marcus shouted. "He is also very smart. Right?"

"Right!" answered Phoebe and Miranda. Noodles rolled over.

He stood up on his hind legs.

He stood up on his front legs.

He did the smartest
tricks he knew.

"I give up," said Leo. "Who is the
perfect mascot?"

Noodles moved to the center
of the clubhouse floor.
What a fine mascot
he would make!

"It's my goldfish, Finny," shouted Marcus.

"It's not Finny," shouted Miranda. "It's my cat, Ralph!"

"It's not Ralph," shouted Phoebe. "It's my parakeet, Mr. Pete!"

Poor Noodles. He wasn't a goldfish or a cat or a parakeet. He was just a shaggy little dog.

Suddenly, the clubhouse was filled
with a delicious smell. A plate of warm
chocolate chip cookies came through the
window.

"These are for taking such good care
of Noodles this morning," said Leo's
dad.

Leo put the plate in the middle of the
clubhouse floor. Each of the Crickets
took a cookie. For a moment, the
clubhouse was quiet.

"That's it!" Leo suddenly shouted.

"What?" asked Miranda.

"A mascot brings good luck, right?" asked Leo.

"So?" said Marcus.

"What about Noodles?" said Leo. "He brought us good luck."

"That's right!" said Miranda. "If it hadn't been for Noodles, we wouldn't be eating these cookies right now."

"Let's take a vote," said Phoebe. "Whoever thinks that Noodles should be our mascot, put your hand up."

Four hands shot up in the air.

"Hooray for Noodles!" the Crickets shouted.

How proud Noodles was! He had walked into the clubhouse that morning just a shaggy little dog.

But he walked out a mascot!

CHAPTER 4

But What Kind of Club Is It?

Marcus and Miranda were walking over to Leo's house for the third meeting of the club.

"There is one thing I don't understand about our club," said Marcus.

"What's that?" asked Miranda.

"We have a name for our club, right?" said Marcus.

"Right," said Miranda.

"And we have a clubhouse and a mascot, right?"

"Right," said Miranda. "So what is the problem?"

"The problem is," said Marcus, "we don't know what kind of club it is."

"Hey, you're right!" said Miranda.

Just then, Miranda saw Phoebe and Leo coming up the street.

"Hey," she called. "We have a problem! We're in a club . . ."

"But we don't know what kind of club we're in," finished Marcus.

"Oh, no!" said Phoebe. "Another problem."

"Let's go into the clubhouse to decide," said Leo.

"Let's take a vote on what kind of club it should be," said Miranda.

"I say it should be a snack club,"
said Marcus.

"What's a snack club?" asked Phoebe.

"Well, you just bring a bunch of snacks
and then you eat them," said Marcus.

"That's dumb," said Phoebe.

"Plus, we don't want ants in our
clubhouse," said Miranda.

"How about a joke club?" said Phoebe.

"Okay," said Miranda. "Someone tell a joke."

"I'll go first," said Marcus. "Why did Leo put the mascot in the refrigerator?"

"Why?" asked Miranda, Leo, and Phoebe.

"Because he wanted a dish of cold noodles. Get it? Noodles is our mascot and . . ."

"Maybe a joke club isn't such a good idea," said Leo.

"I know!" said Miranda. "How about a traveling club?"

"What's a traveling club?" Leo asked.

"You travel to different places and then you write reports about them."

"That's not a traveling club!" said Marcus. "That's a homework club!"

"I'm not going to be in any club that has homework," said Phoebe.

"Okay," said Miranda. "We're not in a traveling club."

"And we're not in a joke club," said Phoebe.

"And we're not in a snack club," said Marcus.

"So what kind of club are we in?" Leo asked.

The clubhouse was silent.

"That does it!" said Marcus. "I'm quitting."

"Me, too," Phoebe said. "I'm not going to be in a club if I don't know what kind of club it is."

For a moment, it seemed that it was the end of the Cool Crazy Crickets.

"Wait!" said Leo, as his friends were crawling out the door. "I know what kind of club it is!"

"You do?" Miranda asked.

"Sure," said Leo. "It's an F. F. L. club!"

"A what?" asked Marcus.

"An F. F. L. club," Leo repeated.

"What does F. F. L. mean?" asked Phoebe. "Four Funny La-dee-das?"

"No," said Leo. "Friends For Life."

"A Friends For Life club?" Marcus said. "That's crazy."

"Right!" Leo said. "But don't forget. We are the Cool *Crazy* Crickets!"

"Look!" Marcus shouted. "I'm a Cricket! I'm a Cool Crazy Cricket!"

"Me, too!" said Miranda.

"Me, three!" said Phoebe.

"Me, four!" said Leo.

"Arf! Arf!" barked Noodles.

And, of course, that's exactly who they were.

LeO   PHOebe
MiRanDa   MaRcuS
NoodLes

Four friends and a mascot.
The Cool Crazy Crickets!
Friends For Life!

THE END